EXTREME MACHINES

MOTORCYCLES

CHRIS OXLADE

A⁺

Smart Apple Media

This book has been published in cooperation with Franklin Watts.

Created for Franklin Watts by Q2A Creative
Editor: Chester Fisher,
Designer: Ashita Murgai,
Picture Researcher: Gautam Trehan

PICTURE CREDITS
Front cover: Honda, Back cover: Honda, pp. 1 main (BMW), 4 top (Yamaha Racing Communications),
5 top (Honda), 5 bottom (Honda), 6 top (David Roosevelt, Ducati Seattle), 7 bottom (BMW), 8 bottom (Honda),
8 middle right (Honda), 9 top (www.harleypics.com), 10 top (Honda), 10 middle right (Honda),
11 middle (Bombardier Recreational Products N.V.), 11 right (Bombardier Recreational Products N.V.),
12 top (Hannigan Motorsports), 12-13 bottom (Superside.com/Rob Mader [Pic:Ian Guy & Andy Peach] Mark
Walters [Pic:Webster & Woodhead] Mark Walters [Pic:Norbury & Parnell]), 14 middle (Fischer Christian),
15 top (Vandenbrink Carver), 16 bottom (www.harleypics.com), 17 top (Confederate Motor Company),
17 bottom (Confederate Motor Company), 18 top (Grant Parsons), 19 bottom (Dennis Tackett Project Manager,
RPM Cycle Dallas, Texas, National Motorcycle Museum Birmingham, England),
20 bottom (National Motor Museum, Beaulieu), 21 top (Mark Elam, All American Cycle, Portland, Oregon),
22 middle (Tom Wiberg, Bigtoe), 22 bottom (Tom Wiberg, Bigtoe), 23 top (Apache, cardesk limited,
Worcestershire, United Kingdom), 23 bottom (Apache, cardesk limited, Worcestershire, United Kingdom),
24 bottom (www.harleypics.com), 25 top (National Motor Museum, Beaulieu), 26 top (David Zatz of Chrysler site
allpar.com), 27 top (David Zatz of Chrysler site allpar.com), 27 bottom (Aprilia Magnet copyright: Heikki Naulapää,
HYPERLINK "http://www.naulapaa.com" www.naulapaa.com), 28 left middle (Science Museum/Science & Society
Picture Library), 28 top middle (Science Museum/Science & Society Picture Library), 28 bottom middle (National
Motor Museum, Beaulieu), 28 to right (National Motor Museum, Beaulieu), 29 middle (National Motor Museum,
Beaulieu), 29 bottom (National Motor Museum, Beaulieu), 31 bottom (Honda)

Published in the United States by Smart Apple Media
2140 Howard Drive West, North Mankato, Minnesota 56003

U.S. publication copyright © 2008 Smart Apple Media
International copyright reserved in all countries. No part of this book may be reproduced in any form
without written permission from the publisher.
Printed in the United States

Library of Congress Cataloging-in-Publication Data

Oxlade, Chris.
Motorcycles / Chris Oxlade.
p. cm. — (Extreme machines)
Includes index.
ISBN-13: 978-1-59920-041-5
1. Motorcycles—Juvenile literature. I. Title.

TL440.15.O95 2007
629.227'5—dc22   2006030844

9 8 7 6 5 4 3 2 1

CONTENTS

RACERS

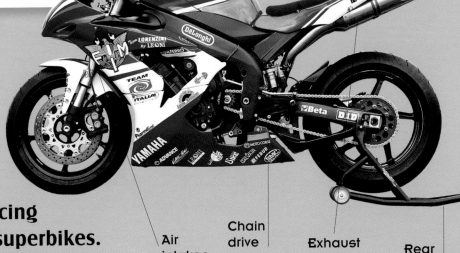

Big engines, terrifying top speeds and high-tech materials; these are the features of the world's biggest racing motorcycles—the superbikes. These machines compete in the World Superbike (WSB) championship. Only expert riders can control their awesome power.

Air intakes

Chain drive

Exhaust silencer

Rear stand

The Yamaha YZF-R1 ready for the race track. It is supported on a rear stand.

TEAM RACER

The Yamaha YZF-R1 is the superbike raced by the riders of the official Yamaha WSB team. With its combination of a light-weight aluminum frame and a powerful engine, it has all the ingredients of a top performer.

FORCED AIR

The Yamaha's engine has a "forced air induction" system for more power. When the bike is moving forward, air is pushed into ducts in the front fairing, forcing air into the engine's cylinders. This allows more fuel to be burned—giving extra power!

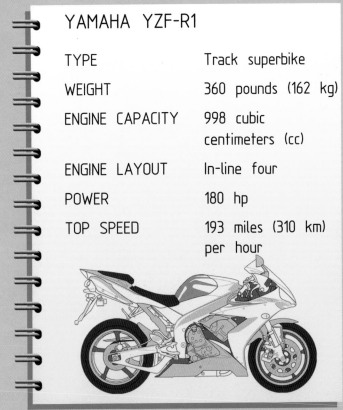

YAMAHA YZF-R1

TYPE	Track superbike
WEIGHT	360 pounds (162 kg)
ENGINE CAPACITY	998 cubic centimeters (cc)
ENGINE LAYOUT	In-line four
POWER	180 hp
TOP SPEED	193 miles (310 km) per hour

HONDA HORSEPOWER

The Honda CBR1000RR Fireblade is the most powerful racing superbike of all. Its four-cylinder engine has a power output of more than 200 horsepower (hp)—that's three times the power of a typical car engine. In the highest gear, it reaches 186 miles (300 km) per hour. That's a staggering 272 feet (83 m) per second! The bike drives in a straight line using an electronically controlled steering damper that prevents the front wheel from wobbling.

The Honda **CBR1000RR** superbike is raced by several of the teams in the World Superbike championship.

HONDA CBR1000RR FIREBLADE

TYPE	Track superbike
WEIGHT	364 pounds (165 kg)
ENGINE CAPACITY	998 cc
ENGINE LAYOUT	In-line four
POWER	200+ hp
TOP SPEED	186 miles (300 km) per hour

web FINDER

http://www.yamaha-racing.com
Site of the official Yamaha WSB team.
http://www.superbike.it
The Superbike World championship official site.

998-cc engine

Front disc brakes

STREET SUPERBIKES

Superbikes are not just for racing on the track. Most are also manufactured in street-ready versions. These have all the extras needed to make them "street legal," such as mirrors and registration plates, as well as state-of-the-art technology borrowed from track racers.

Six-speed gearbox

Polymer fairing

The Ducati 999 Testastretta has a lightweight frame made of steel tubes welded together.

DUCATI 999 TESTASTRETTA

TYPE	Street-ready superbike
WEIGHT	410 pounds (186 kg)
ENGINE CAPACITY	998 cc
ENGINE LAYOUT	L-twin
POWER	124 hp
TOP SPEED	168 miles (270 km) per hour

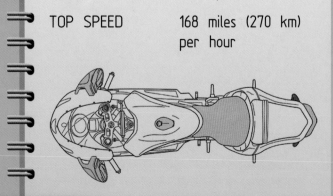

DREAM DUCATI

Ducati is the Ferrari of the motorcycle world. The stunning Ducati 999 Testastretta is Ducati's most high-performance and technically advanced bike. It is the dream bike of most motorcycle enthusiasts. The twin-cylinder Testastretta engine was developed for the track and pushes the bike to a top speed of 168 miles (270 km) per hour.

The BMW K1200S is one of the few superbikes to feature a front suspension arm instead of straight suspension forks.

SHAFT DRIVE BIKE

The BMW K1200S is the most powerful superbike that BMW has ever built. It borrows engine technology from BMW's Formula One car engines. The engine can accelerate the bike from a standstill to 62 miles (100 km) per hour in just 2.8 seconds. A unique feature of the K1200S is the lightweight shaft drive that carries power from the engine to the rear wheel. Other superbikes have a chain drive, which is a heavier system.

Indicators in mirrors

Front suspension arm

Alloy wheels

BMW K1200S

TYPE	Street-ready superbike
WEIGHT	547 pounds (248 kg)
ENGINE CAPACITY	1,157 cc
ENGINE LAYOUT	In-line four
POWER	167 hp
TOP SPEED	124 miles (200 km) per hour

web

FINDER

http://www.ducati.com
Official Ducati Web site.
http://www.bmw.com
Official BMW Web site.

ON TOUR

Touring bikes are the giants of the motorcycle world. They are built for comfort on long-distance journeys, but that doesn't make them slow! Tourers have a passenger seat, luggage space, and lots of gadgets.

KING OF THE ROAD

The Honda Gold Wing is the most famous touring bike in the world. The first Gold Wing was made in 1975. Its monstrous six-cylinder, 1,832-cc engine is more powerful than most car engines. The Gold Wing features advanced gadgets such as an electric motor for reversing, cruise control, computer-controlled suspension, and ABS brakes for safer braking.

The Honda Gold Wing is an impressive 8.66 feet (2.64 m) long. Its six-cylinder engine drives the rear wheel using a shaft.

HONDA GOLD WING

TYPE	Big tourer
WEIGHT	800 pounds (363 kg)
ENGINE CAPACITY	1,832 cc
ENGINE LAYOUT	Horizontally opposed six
POWER	117 hp
TOP SPEED	118 miles (190 km) per hour

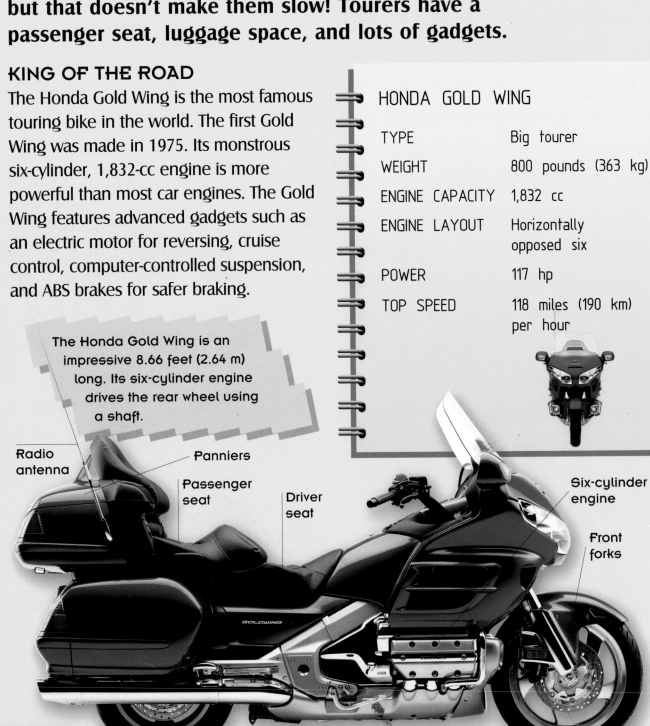

Radio antenna

Panniers

Passenger seat

Driver seat

Six-cylinder engine

Front forks

Exhaust
pipe

Panniers

Passenger
seat

V-twin
engine

The Harley-Davidson Road Glide
is the company's latest giant
touring machine.

STREET GLIDER

The Harley-Davidson FLTRI Road Glide is the
latest big touring bike from the famous
American manufacturer. Like all of Harley-
Davidson's big bikes, it is powered by a 1,450 cc,
V-twin engine. That means it has two giant
cylinders arranged in a V shape. The engine
makes a throaty, throbbing roar that sounds
like no other engine! It is only drowned out
by the bike's 40-watt stereo hi-fi speakers.

FINDER

http://www.powersports.honda.com/motorcycles
Official site of Honda motorcycles.
http://www.harley-davidson.com
Official site of Harley-Davidson motorcycles.

HARLEY-DAVIDSON FLTRI ROAD GLIDE

TYPE	Tourer
WEIGHT	732 pounds (332 kg)
ENGINE CAPACITY	1,450 cc
ENGINE LAYOUT	V-twin
POWER	67 hp
TOP SPEED	110 miles (175 km) per hour

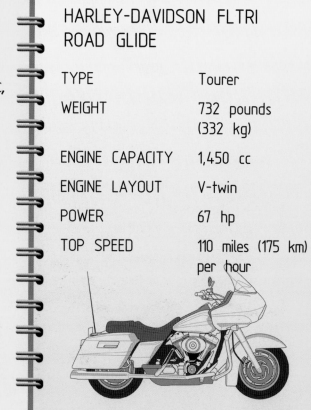

DIRT BIKES

Protective
skid plate

Suspension
springs

Motorcycles designed for traveling across the countryside feature super-strong suspensions to cope with bumpy ground and chunky tires to grip the mud. They are used for cross-country racing and for transportation on farms.

The Honda CRF 450R powers into the air in a freestyle jumping competition.

MOTOCROSS MOTOR

The Honda CRF 450R is possibly the best dirt bike in the world. The powerful 450-cc engine effortlessly moves it through dirt and mud and is a popular choice for motocross riders, stunt riders, and rally riders. The front suspension springs and rear shock absorption squeeze together or "travel" by more than 12 inches (30 cm) to absorb bone-crunching landings after jumps.

HONDA CRF 450R

TYPE	Dirt bike
WEIGHT	218 pounds (99 kg)
ENGINE CAPACITY	450 cc
ENGINE LAYOUT	Single
POWER	55 hp
TOP SPEED	81 miles (130 km) per hour

FOUR-WHEEL RACER

A quad bike is a motorcycle with four wheels instead of the usual two. Quad bikes feature motorcycle-style engines, frames, and suspensions. The Bombardier DS650 Baja is a sports quad and the fastest quad bike around, with a top speed of 75 miles (120 km) per hour. The DS650 was also the only quad bike to complete the gruelling 6,835 mile (11,000 km) Dakar Rally in 2004.

Motorcycle-style controls on handlebars

Skid plate

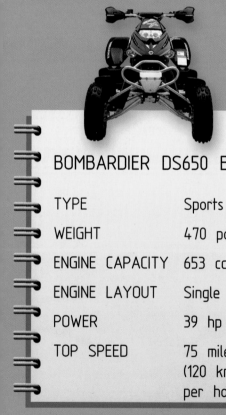

BOMBARDIER DS650 BAJA

TYPE	Sports quad bike
WEIGHT	470 pounds (213 kg)
ENGINE CAPACITY	653 cc
ENGINE LAYOUT	Single
POWER	39 hp
TOP SPEED	75 miles (120 km) per hour

web

FINDER

http://www.honda.co.uk/motorcycles
Official site of Honda motorcycles.
http://www.bombardier-atv.com/enUS/Vehicles/2005/DS650
Details of the Bombardier quad bike.

The Bombardier DS650 features independent suspension on each wheel.

SIDECARS

The Hannigan GTL features electronic controls to keep the bike upright.

Fiberglass-reinforced plastic body shell

Honda Gold Wing

Foot plate

A sidecar is a small passenger compartment attached to the side of a motorcycle. Sidecars are normally bolted onto touring bikes, but there are racing sidecars, too. A motorcycle and sidecar combination cannot tip like a motorcycle on its own can.

HANNIGAN GTL

TYPE	Touring sidecar
WEIGHT	276 pounds (125 kg)
LOAD CAPACITY	353 pounds (160 kg)
LENGTH	7.5 feet (2.3 m)
WIDTH	3.6 feet (1.1 m)

LUXURY TRAVEL

Touring sidecars are designed to carry a passenger and luggage. The sleek sidecar, the Hannigan GTL, is purpose-built for the giant Honda Gold Wing touring bike. Inside is a reclining bucket seat with a headrest. Its aerodynamic shape creates a downforce that presses its tires onto the road for extra grip. A hard top or soft top protects the passenger from the rain.

Passenger

RACING SIDECAR

The fastest sidecars in the world are the Formula One racing sidecars that take part in the World Sidecar Championship. These machines have a low motorcycle along one side, with a third wheel to the side. The entire machine is covered with a fairing to make it aerodynamic. Combined with the 1,000-cc superbike engine, this allows speeds up to 180 miles (290 km) per hour.

A Formula One racing sidecar taking a right-hand corner at top speed.

FORMULA ONE SIDECAR BIKE

TYPE	Racing sidecar bike
WEIGHT	827 pounds (375 kg)
ENGINE CAPACITY	1,000 cc
ENGINE LAYOUT	In-line four
POWER	180 hp
TOP SPEED	112 miles (180 km) per hour

SIDECAR DRIVING

A sidecar has a team of two—a rider and a passenger. To prevent the sidecar from flipping over sideways on corners, the passenger throws his weight over the wheel on the inside of the bend. This keeps the wheel on the ground.

web

FINDER

http://www.hannigansidecar.com
Web site of the U.S. sidecar maker.
http://www.superside.com
Web site of the World Sidecar Championship.

Driver

TRIKES

A tricycle, or trike, is a motorcycle with three wheels instead of two. Most trikes have one front and two rear wheels. Trikes are easier and safer to ride than two-wheelers and are a popular choice for touring and cruising.

SPORTS TRIKE

The Triketec V-2 Roadster is a purpose-built two-seater sports trike. Its long handlebar and low seats give it the look of a giant "chopper" bike. The 698-cc turbocharged engine and six-speed gearbox gives a fun and exciting ride. It includes high-tech features such as anti-lock brakes.

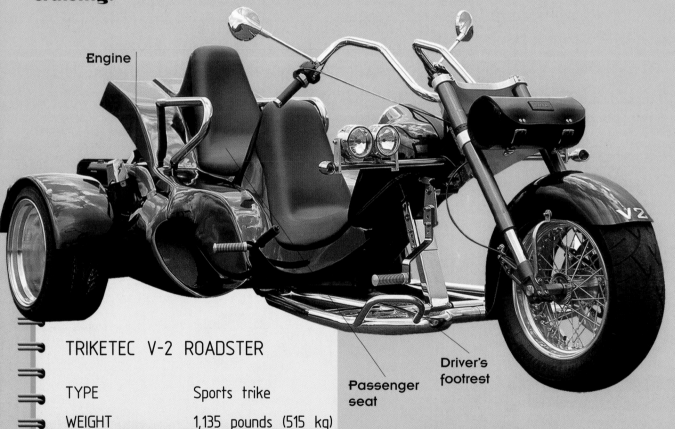

Engine

Passenger seat

Driver's footrest

TRIKETEC V-2 ROADSTER

TYPE	Sports trike
WEIGHT	1,135 pounds (515 kg)
ENGINE CAPACITY	689 cc
ENGINE LAYOUT	In-line three
POWER	82 hp
TOP SPEED	106 miles (170 km) per hour

The Triketec V-2 Roadster has its engine at the back, between the two rear wheels.

The Vandenbrink Carver has a complex leaning system.

Body leans over

Rear chassis stays level in corner

BIKE OR CAR?

From the inside, the extraordinary Vandenbrink Carver looks like a tiny car. There's a wheel for steering and a lever for shifting gears, but when the Carver takes a corner, the body leans over like a cornering motorcycle. The amount it leans is controlled automatically. In sharper turns and at higher speeds, the machine leans more. The maximum lean is 45 degrees.

web

FINDER
www.triketec.com
Site of the Triketec company.
www.carver.nl
The Dutch manufacturer of the Vandenbrink Carver.

VANDENBRINK CARVER

TYPE	Motorcycle/car hybrid
WEIGHT	1,411 pounds (640 kg)
ENGINE CAPACITY	660-cc turbo
ENGINE LAYOUT	In-line four
POWER	65 hp
TOP SPEED	115 miles (185 km) per hour

CHOPPERS

In the 1950s, American motorcycle enthusiasts began to customize their Harley-Davidson bikes. To reduce weight and improve performance, they chopped off any parts they did not need. Typical features of modern "choppers" are long front forks and a low-slung seat.

CLASSIC STYLE

The Big Dog Chopper is a modern chopper with classic chopper looks. Power from the 1,916-cc engine is sent to the fat rear tire, which is 9.8 inches (25 cm) across. The chopper measures an incredible 8.66 feet (2.64 m) from end to end.

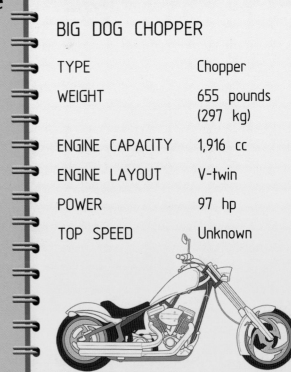

BIG DOG CHOPPER

TYPE	Chopper
WEIGHT	655 pounds (297 kg)
ENGINE CAPACITY	1,916 cc
ENGINE LAYOUT	V-twin
POWER	97 hp
TOP SPEED	Unknown

A chopper bike made by customizing a Harley-Davidson motorcycle.

V-TWIN POWER

Like all choppers, the Big Dog machine is powered by a giant V-twin engine. This is the type of engine that all the original Harley-Davidson choppers had. The V-twin is the classic American big-bike engine.

BEAST FROM NEW ORLEANS

The Confederate Hellcat doesn't have the looks of a classic chopper, but is "chopped" down to the bone. There are no unnecessary ornaments on this bike. Every Hellcat is hand-built from modern materials such as carbon fiber, aircraft-grade aluminum and high-tensile steel.

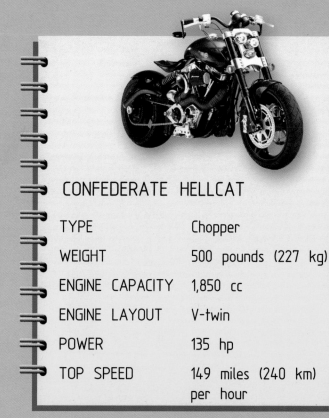

CONFEDERATE HELLCAT

TYPE	Chopper
WEIGHT	500 pounds (227 kg)
ENGINE CAPACITY	1,850 cc
ENGINE LAYOUT	V-twin
POWER	135 hp
TOP SPEED	149 miles (240 km) per hour

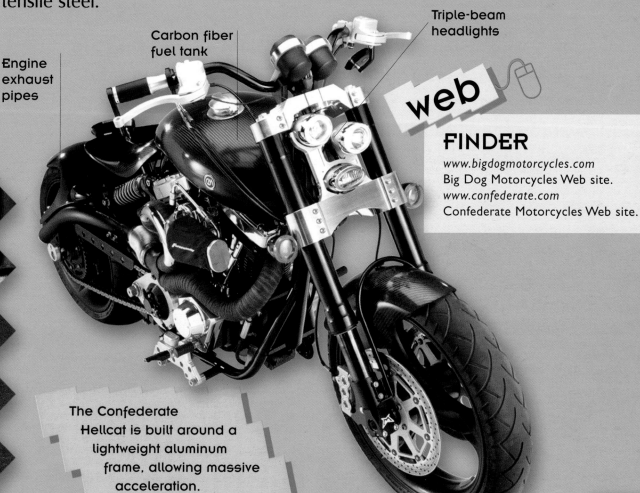

Engine exhaust pipes

Carbon fiber fuel tank

Triple-beam headlights

The Confederate Hellcat is built around a lightweight aluminum frame, allowing massive acceleration.

web

FINDER

www.bigdogmotorcycles.com
Big Dog Motorcycles Web site.
www.confederate.com
Confederate Motorcycles Web site.

THE FASTEST

The record-holding EZ-Hook Streamliner has a tail like an airplane to keep it going in a straight line.

You might know about the world land-speed record for cars, but there is also a motorcycle, or two-wheeled, world land-speed record held by the fastest motorcycle on the planet! Many extraordinary and bizarre machines have been built to try to break this record.

RECORD HOLDER

The holder of the motorcycle world land-speed record for wheel-driven motorcycles is called the EZ-Hook Streamliner. Wheel-driven means that the engine makes the wheels turn, and drives the machine forward. It set the record of 334 miles (537.6 km) per hour in 2003. A streamliner is a bike that is completely covered with a streamlined aerodynamic fairing. This reduces air resistance. The EZ-Hook is powered by the engine from a Kawasaki superbike.

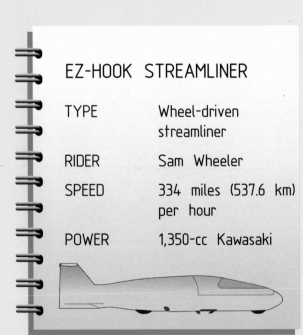

EZ-HOOK STREAMLINER	
TYPE	Wheel-driven streamliner
RIDER	Sam Wheeler
SPEED	334 miles (537.6 km) per hour
POWER	1,350-cc Kawasaki

TRIUMPH STREAMLINER

A streamliner powered by the engine from a Triumph motorcycle broke the motorcycle world speed record in 1956. It reached a top speed of 214 miles (345 km) per hour. The engine burned a mixture of methanol and nitrous oxide fuel. The bike set the record at Bonneville Salt Flats in Utah.

STREAMLINER REBORN!

In 2003, the record-breaking streamliner, nicknamed the Texas Ceegar, was almost destroyed by a disastrous fire at the National Motorcycle Museum in the United Kingdom (UK). A team of enthusiasts in Texas accepted the challenge of rebuilding it. The restored streamliner was raced again at Bonneville before being returned for display at the museum.

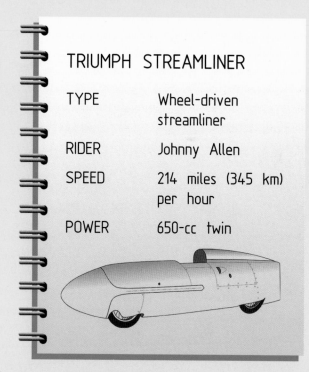

TRIUMPH STREAMLINER

TYPE	Wheel-driven streamliner
RIDER	Johnny Allen
SPEED	214 miles (345 km) per hour
POWER	650-cc twin

web

FINDER

www.speedtrialsbybub.com
News, information, photos, and videos of motorcycle speed trials on the Bonneville Salt Flats.
www.streamliner.com
The EZ-Hook streamliner Web site.

The Triumph Streamliner standing on the Bonneville Salt Flats, where it set the motorcycle world speed record in 1956.

Engine compartment cover

Rider cockpit

DRAG RACERS

Drag-bike races are short but incredibly fast! The bikes race in pairs along a 1,300 foot (400 m) straight track. Drag bikes have giant rear tires that drive them down the track in a cloud of rubbery smoke. They are still accelerating when they reach the finish and need parachutes to slow down again.

FUNNY BIKE

Funny bikes are one of the types, or classes, of bikes that take part in drag-bike racing. American funny bikes must have a 12-inch (30 cm) rear tire and wheels that are 7.2 feet (2.2 m) apart. They consume regular unleaded gasoline. The rider can also add a chemical called nitrous oxide into the cylinders for an extra boost of power.

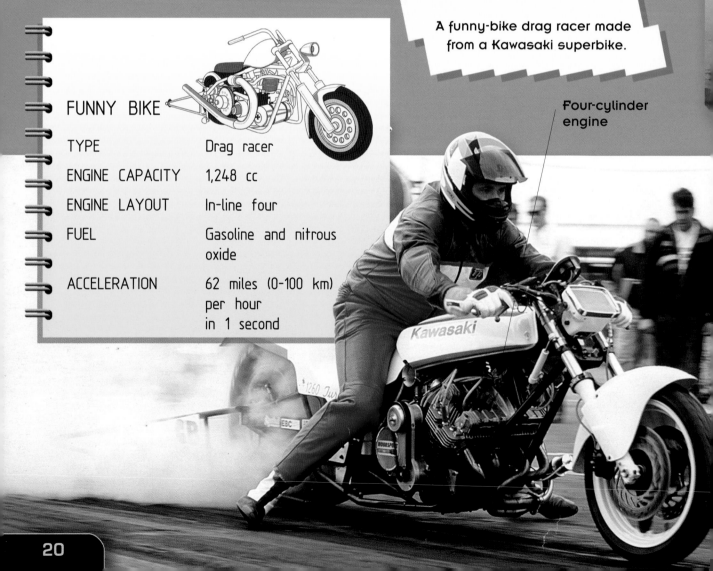

A funny-bike drag racer made from a Kawasaki superbike.

Four-cylinder engine

FUNNY BIKE

TYPE	Drag racer
ENGINE CAPACITY	1,248 cc
ENGINE LAYOUT	In-line four
FUEL	Gasoline and nitrous oxide
ACCELERATION	62 miles (0-100 km) per hour in 1 second

Smoke pours from the spinning rear wheel of a nitro-methane-powered top fuel bike.

Safety bar stops the bike from flipping over backwards

Giant rear tire

TOP FUEL BIKE

Drag bikes in the top fuel class burn a special fuel called nitromethane. It is the type of fuel used in rockets! It gives much more energy than gasoline. Top fuel engines produce massive power, making the bikes the most powerful and the fastest of all drag bikes. A top fuel engine gulps down up to 4 gallons (20 l) of nitromethane in one race.

TOP FUEL BIKE

TYPE	Drag racer
ENGINE CAPACITY	1,400 cc
ENGINE LAYOUT	V-twin
FUEL	Nitromethane
ACCELERATION	62 miles (0-100 km) per hour in 0.8 seconds

web

FINDER
www.dragbike.com
On-line drag-bike racing magazine.

BIG AND SMALL

There are hundreds of medium-sized motorcycles—some small motorcycles and some big motorcycles, a few tiny motorcycles and a few giant motorcycles! The world's smallest working bike is just four inches (10cm) long! And yes, it can be ridden!

THE TALLEST

The world's tallest motorcycle is called Bigtoe. This monster bike is 7.5 feet (2.3 m) high and 15.4 feet (4.7 m) long. Bigtoe was completed in 1998 by Swedish bike enthusiast Tom Wiberg, after five years of work. He included a V-12 engine from a Jaguar sports car, giving it a top speed of 62 miles (100 km) per hour. The music system consists of four 500-watt speakers.

BIGTOE	
TYPE	World's tallest motorcycle
WEIGHT	3,627 pounds (1,645 kg)
ENGINE CAPACITY	6,000 cc
ENGINE LAYOUT	V-12
POWER	300 hp
TOP SPEED	62 miles (100 km) per hour

V-12, 6,000-cc engine

Tom Wiberg

Hydraulic suspension

Structural frame

The Apache PY50 looks like an adult bike, but is only half as high.

49-cc engine

CHILD'S PLAY

The Apache PY50 is like a shrunken full-size dirt bike. It's designed for small children to ride around their yards and cross-country. Although every part is miniature, the bike is still exciting to ride. Miniature bikes like the PY50 are called mini motos or pocket bikes. They are not just for children—there are popular mini moto racing competitions for adults!

Bigtoe is taller, heavier, and more powerful than any other motorcycle.

APACHE PY50	
TYPE	Children's cross-country
WEIGHT	55 pounds (25 kg)
ENGINE CAPACITY	49 cc
ENGINE LAYOUT	Single
POWER	3 hp
TOP SPEED	22 miles (35 km) per hour

web FINDER

http:/biphome.spray.se/bigtoe/
Bigtoe home page.
www.minimoto.com
Mini-motorcycle racing site.

CLASSICS

The best motorcycles of the past are known as classic bikes. The first classic motorcycles were made more than 100 years ago. Classics might look old now, but they were cutting-edge machines when they were designed. Motorcycle enthusiasts collect these machines and lovingly restore them.

FIGHTING HARLEY

The Harley-Davidson 45 is a classic American motorcycle that was manufactured by the famous Harley-Davidson company in the 1930s and 1940s. An amazing 88,000 Harley-Davidson bikes were made for the Allied armies in World War II. The rugged machine was used by dispatch riders carrying messages. After the war, thousands of ex-servicemen bought the bikes and converted them to street bikes.

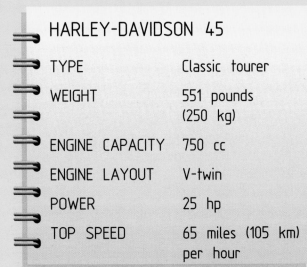

HARLEY-DAVIDSON 45	
TYPE	Classic tourer
WEIGHT	551 pounds (250 kg)
ENGINE CAPACITY	750 cc
ENGINE LAYOUT	V-twin
POWER	25 hp
TOP SPEED	65 miles (105 km) per hour

This Harley-Davidson 45 is more than 50 years old. It has been carefully restored by its owner.

Fuel tank

Frame

Cylinders of V-twin engine

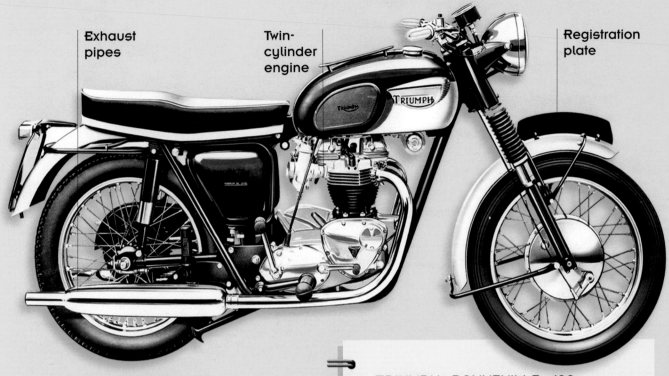

Exhaust pipes

Twin-cylinder engine

Registration plate

The original Triumph 120 was tough and reliable, as well as very fast.

INTO THE FUTURE

The Triumph Bonneville 120 was built by the British motorcycle company Triumph. The bike was named after the Bonneville Salt Flats in Utah where a motorcycle powered by a Triumph engine broke the motorcycle world land-speed record in 1956 (see page 19). The "120" stood for 120 miles (193 km) per hour, the Bonneville's top speed, making it one of the quickest bikes of the time. In 2001, the Bonneville was relaunched with a modern version. This retains the feel and the spirit of the original with easy-handling chassis and lean, classical styling, but has many modern features as well.

TRIUMPH BONNEVILLE 120

TYPE	Classic superbike
WEIGHT	441 pounds (200 kg)
ENGINE CAPACITY	649 cc
ENGINE LAYOUT	Parallel twin
POWER	50 hp
TOP SPEED	120 miles (190 km) per hour

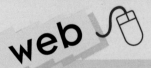

FINDER

www.harley-davidson.com
Official Harley-Davidson site includes excellent section on the company's classic bikes.
www.triumph.co.uk
For details of the modern Bonneville.

CONCEPTS

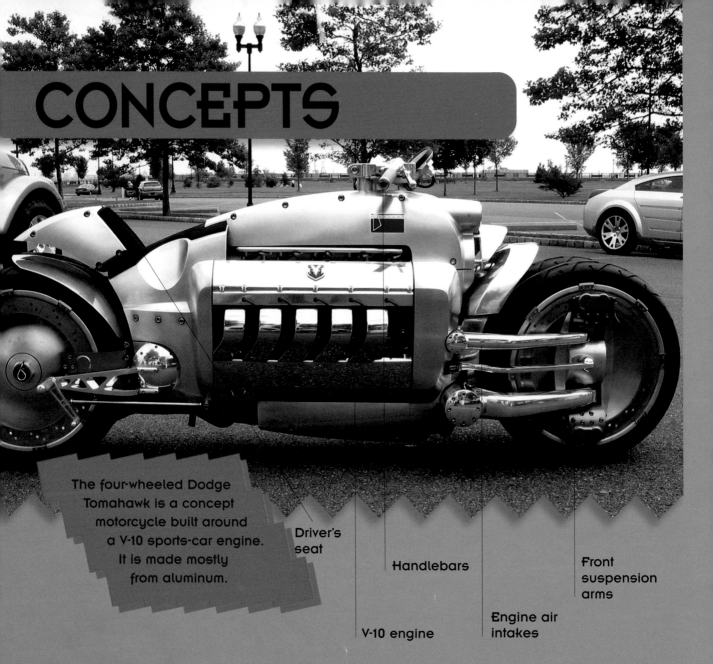

The four-wheeled Dodge Tomahawk is a concept motorcycle built around a V-10 sports-car engine. It is made mostly from aluminum.

Driver's seat

Handlebars

Front suspension arms

Engine air intakes

V-10 engine

What will the motorcycles of the future look like? Concept bikes give us an idea. These are designed by motorcycle manufacturers to show off new technical ideas. Most only exist on paper, but some are built for motorcycle shows.

SILVER MACHINE

The extraordinary Dodge Tomahawk concept bike is twice as powerful as a top superbike. Despite weighing as much as a small car, it can reach 62 miles (100 km) per hour in 2.5 seconds! Its V-10 engine comes from a Dodge Viper sports car. There is so much power that the bike needs two wheels at each end, with independent suspension in each.

DODGE TOMAHAWK

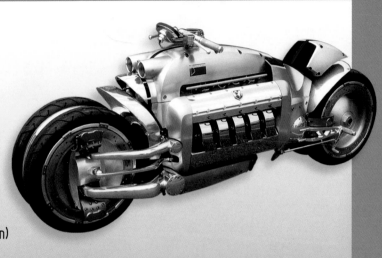

TYPE	Concept bike
WEIGHT	1,499 pounds (680 kg)
ENGINE CAPACITY	8,277 cc
ENGINE LAYOUT	V-10
POWER	500 hp
TOP SPEED	311 miles (500 km) plus per hour

HUBLESS MAGNET

The Aprilia Magnet concept bike was designed for the Italian motorcycle manufacturer Aprilia. It is a trike with two-wheel steering at the front and a tilting mechanism for the body. The rider almost lies down to steer. The wheels have no hubs and are driven by electric motors on their rims. The electricity comes from a generator driven by a 550-cc engine.

web

FINDER

www.aprilia.com/magnet.asp
Computer models of the Aprilia Magnet.
www.allpar.com/cars/concepts/tomahawk.html
Technical details on the Tomahawk.

Front suspension spring

Electric motors

Driver's controls

V-10 engine

The Aprilia Magnet concept trike's engine drives a generator that provides electricity to electric motors on the wheels.

TIMELINE

1838

Scottish blacksmith Kirkpatrick Macmillan builds one of the first bicycles with pedals that the rider pushes backward and forward to propel it along. The first motorcycles are really just bicycles with engines.

1869

The Michaux-Perreaux motorcycle is the first bicycle powered with a steam engine. The hot engine is under the driver's seat! Several other steam-powered motorcycles are built at this time. The Michaux-Perreaux machine is the first motorcycle.

1876

German engineer Gottlieb Daimler invents the four-stroke internal combustion engine, using petrol as fuel. This is the type of engine used in most modern motorcycles.

1885

British engineer John Starley invents his "safety" bicycle, featuring a diamond-shaped frame, a chain drive, and brakes.

1885

Gottlieb Daimler builds a motorcycle powered by one of his gasoline engines, a 264-cc model. It has a wooden frame and small stabilizing wheels on each side because it is heavy and unsteady.

1894

The first production motorcycle, the Hildebrand & Wolfmuller, begins to be made in Germany (earlier bikes were one-of-a-kind machines).

1901

In France, the Werner brothers build a machine with the engine at the bottom of the frame. This is the layout used in all modern motorcycles.

1903

The Harley-Davidson company is formed in the U.S. by William, Walter, and Arthur Davidson and William Harley. Their first motorcycle is built in 1904.

1903

The motorcycle sidecar is invented.

1905

The chain drive is introduced to motorcycles. Before this, the engine drove the rear wheel with a leather belt.

1907

The first of the famous Isle of Man TT races takes place. The races are still running today.

1907

The world's first proper motorcycle-racing (and car-racing) track, with huge banked corners, was built at Brooklands in the UK.

1914
The first motorcycle trail race, the Scott Trial, is held in Yorkshire, UK.

1920
Speedway racing (racing on an oval-shaped dirt track) is developed in the U.S.

1923
BMW launches its first motorcycle, the 500-cc R32.

1929
Harley-Davidson builds the first Harley-Davidson 45.

1935
BMW introduces the telescopic fork on the front suspension of its motorcycles. This is a feature of most modern motorcycles.

1939–45
Motorcycles play an important role in World War II. They are used mainly by dispatch riders, but also serve as machine-gun platforms, with the gun in the sidecar.

1948
The Honda motorcycle company is formed in Japan. Honda now makes more motorcycles than any other manufacturer.

1948
The Vincent Black Shadow is the first motorcycle to travel 155 miles (250 km) per hour.

1950
American bike enthusiasts begin building the first "choppers" from Harley-Davidson motorcycles.

1958
The Honda Super Cub with its 50-cc engine begins production. It becomes the biggest-selling motorcycle ever.

1959
Triumph begins production of the Bonneville 120.

1968
The Honda CB750 causes a sensation when launched at the Tokyo Motorcycle Show. It is the first motorcycle to be called a "superbike."

1968
Italian rider Giacomo Agostini wins the first of five successive Isle of Man TT races on his MV Augusta machine.

1974
American stunt rider Evel Knievel attempts to jump a canyon on a trials motorcycle. He doesn't make it and parachutes to safety.

1975
The first Honda Gold Wing with a 1,000-cc engine, is produced.

1988
The first World Superbike championship is held.

1990
The Easy Riders streamliner breaks the motorcycle world speed record.

1992
Honda launches its Fireblade superbike.

2003
EZ-Hook breaks the motorcycle world speed record at Bonneville Salt Flats in Utah.

GLOSSARY

CAPACITY

The volume inside the cylinders of an engine. The bigger the capacity, the more power the engine produces.

CC

Short for "cubic centimeter," a measure of the capacity of an engine.

CHOPPER

Motorcycle stripped down to its essential parts with no decoration.

CYLINDER

Space inside an engine in which the fuel is burned to make pistons move in and out.

DAMPER

Device that reduces (or damps down) vibrations.

EXHAUST

System of pipes at the rear of a motorcycle, for carrying waste gases from the engine into the air.

FAIRING

Smooth cover over a motorcycle frame that allows air to flow smoothly over the bike.

FRONT FORKS

Struts that connect a motorcycle's front wheel to its frame.

HORSEPOWER (HP)

A measure of the energy output (or power) of an engine.

IN-LINE ENGINE

Arrangement in which the cylinders are arranged parallel to each other in a line.

L-TWIN ENGINE

Arrangement in which the two cylinders are arranged at right angles to each other.

PARALLEL TWIN ENGINE

Arrangement in which two cylinders are next to each other.

QUAD

Motorcycle with four wheels.

SHAFT DRIVE

Spinning rod that carries power from a motorcycle's engine to its rear.

SHOCK ABSORBER

Part of a suspension system that soaks up the energy if a bike hits a violent bump.

SIDECAR

Small passenger compartment attached to the side of a motorcycle.

SINGLE-ENGINE ARRANGEMENT

An engine with just one cylinder.

SUPERBIKE

Lightweight motorcycle with powerful engine and excellent performance for track racing and sports riding.

SUSPENSION

System that connects a motorcycle's wheels and frame, allowing the wheels to move up and down over bumps.

THROTTLE

Twisting handle that changes the amount of fuel reaching the engine and the power coming from the engine.

TRIKE

Motorcycle with three wheels.

TURBOCHARGER

Device that blows air into an engine's cylinders, allowing it to burn more fuel and produce more power.

V-10 OR V-12 ENGINE

Arrangement in which 10 or 12 cylinders are arranged in two rows at an angle to each other.

V-TWIN ENGINE

Arrangement in which two cylinders are arranged at an angle to each other, making a V-shape.

WHEEL

Cruise control that makes a motorcycle travel at constant speed automatically. Allows the rider to release the throttle.

Note to parents and teachers:
Every effort has been made to ensure that the Web sites in this book are suitable for children, that they are of the highest educational value, and that they contain no inappropriate or offensive material. However, because of the nature of the Internet, it is impossible to guarantee that the contents of these sites will not be altered. We strongly advise that Internet access be supervised by a responsible adult.

INDEX